Squish Rabbit

Katherine Battersby

VIKING

An Imprint of Penguin Group (USA) Inc.

Squish was just a little rabbit.
But being little led to big problems.

Sometimes Squish was
hard to see.

(Which is how he got his name.)

Wonderful things . . .

passed him by.

No one noticed Squish,
or listened to his stories.

Being little was lonely.

So Squish made a friend.

It worked for a while.

But pretend friends
can only do so much.

Squish tried playing
with the trees instead.

But they broke
all the rules.

Squish thought no one was watching,
so he threw a little tantrum.

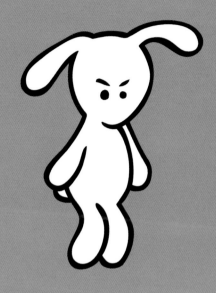

He kicked his little legs,
but someone thought he was playing.

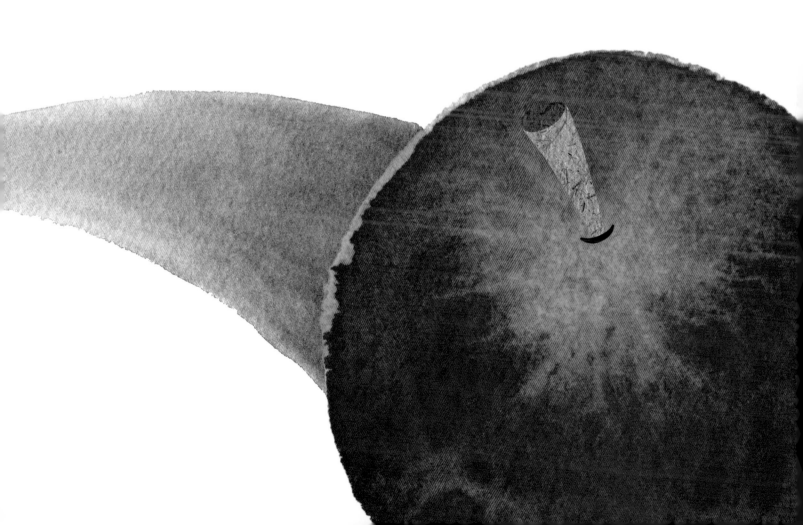

Squish watched with wide little eyes.

The squirrel bounded on, and
Squish's heart skipped a little beat.

Squish waved his little arms,
opened his little mouth, and . . .

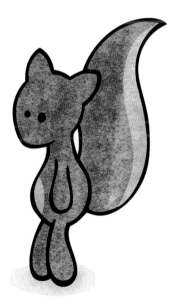

Squish was just a little rabbit,
but his friends made him feel much bigger.

For Andrew, another rabbit with
big and beautiful things inside him.

VIKING
Published by Penguin Group
Penguin Young Readers Group, 345 Hudson Street, New York, New York 10014, U.S.A.
Penguin Group (Canada), 90 Eglinton Avenue East, Suite 700, Toronto, Ontario, Canada M4P 2Y3
(a division of Pearson Penguin Canada Inc.)
Penguin Books Ltd, 80 Strand, London WC2R 0RL, England
Penguin Ireland, 25 St Stephen's Green, Dublin 2, Ireland
(a division of Penguin Books Ltd)
Penguin Group (Australia), 250 Camberwell Road, Camberwell, Victoria 3124, Australia
(a division of Pearson Australia Group Pty Ltd)
Penguin Books India Pvt Ltd, 11 Community Centre, Panchsheel Park, New Delhi – 110 017, India
Penguin Group (NZ), 67 Apollo Drive, Rosedale, North Shore 0632, New Zealand
(a division of Pearson New Zealand Ltd.)
Penguin Books (South Africa) (Pty) Ltd, 24 Sturdee Avenue, Rosebank, Johannesburg 2196, South Africa

Penguin Books Ltd, Registered Offices: 80 Strand, London WC2R 0RL, England

First published in 2011 by Viking, a division of Penguin Young Readers Group

1   3   5   7   9   10   8   6   4   2

LIBRARY OF CONGRESS CATALOGING-IN-PUBLICATION DATA IS AVAILABLE
ISBN 978-0-670-01267-1

Manufactured in China   Set in Cochin Medium